Country Fair

ELISHA COOPER

Greenwillow Books  New York

There is a field outside of town. It's wide and rolling, with clumps of trees,

dirt road

a dirt road at one end, and blue hills that watch over everything.

Today, early in the morning, the field is empty.

blue hill

Then tractors and trailers rumble in and fill the field with honks and slamming doors.

Farmers and animals get out of their trucks and stretch their legs.

Canvas tents rise from the ground like wind-filled sails.

Workers swing from ropes, tie knots,

and hang upside down. One man loses his balance

and tumbles into a pile of hay.

Sheep get brushed, clipped, picked over for bits of dirt,

and covered with blankets to keep them clean. A ram

whose horns curl twice around his ears waits his turn.

A cow enjoys her morning bath. She has dark eyes and long

lashes that blink away soapsuds. When she's dry, a neighbor

almost drops a cowpie on her, but a farmer moves her just in time.

A sow gets loose. She looks like a pink refrigerator with legs, and when she runs, people get out of the way. It takes ten minutes, five waving farmers, three buckets

of grain, and one push on the rump to coax her back to her pen.

A judge with small glasses sits at a table.

She cuts a slice of banana bread, sniffs it,

holds it up to the light, pokes it, prods it, and bites.

She chews thoughtfully, then scribbles notes.

At the vegetable weigh-in, three men wrestle uncooperative pumpkins.

They look like clumsy giants grappling hot-air balloons. When they pin one on the scale, they give each other high fives and a pat on the back.

Lunchtime. A cook prepares three hamburgers, two sodas, one sausage, a side of fries, fried dough, chees

curds, a root beer float, an ice cream sundae, and a hot apple pie – all for one big man in overalls. A yellow jacket helps him eat.

At the afternoon cattle show, a judge with a ponytail studies the cows. They study her. Farmers try to keep their cows still, while the cows try to drool on their farmers. The cow voted "Most Original" eats her ribbon.

The sow who ran away and came back is judged "Prettiest Pig." She snores contentedly and shares the blue ribbon with her five piglets, taking care not to roll over.

A bald man shears sheep. He bends them this way and

and can't find their towels.

and naked, as if they've just stepped out of the shower

that as if he were folding laundry, but the sheep don't mind, and

huge clumps of wool fall to the ground.

When the sheep are done, they look clean and pink

CATTLE

SWINE

A tufty rooster sprints up the side of his cage and hangs from the top.

Rabbits with rumpled fur twitch and quiver as if they're about to sneeze.

A goat who smells like old sneakers curls his lip and chews his cud.

A frowning llama stands by herself and looks angry and ready to spit.

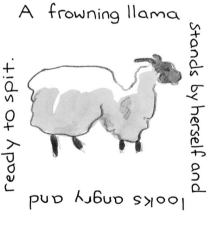

A bristly-haired, striped pig named Slim mucks around in a bucket of muck.

A horse scans the front page, then nibbles through the comics section.

Heaving and straining, lowing and puffing, they're urged on by shouts of "Gee! Haw!" as their owners try to pull six thousand-pound concrete blocks. Oxen teams named Blue & Babe, Babe & Bud, Bud & Bill, and Bert & Ernie

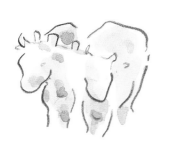

"Haw!" and "Whoop!" When a team pulls the weight successfully, the other oxen waggle their ears.

In the bicycle-tractor pull, a driver keeps pedaling until the weight gets too heavy.

In the corn-shucking contest, a girl creates a storm of husks and flying yellow fuzz.

The winner of the pie-eating contest tries to hug a friend who doesn't feel quite as friendly.

The duck who wins the Great Duck Race is the only one who goes the right way.

A burly man in metal sandals slices through a board with four quick, diagonal strokes.

At the wood-chopping exhibition, a woman hurls her ax into the target with a "thunk."

A man balances a board on his head, then a canoe, then a nervous woman named Nan.

Two sweaty cutters grunt as they push and pull and yank a saw through a tree.

Shadows lengthen and fair-goers ride around and around. A juggler sways back and forth

On a unicycle, juggling fire, then eating it. He washes it down with a chocolate milk shake.

A man with long legs stomps by,

while a pair of puppets dance and sing with each other.

They bob their heads, jab the air with each note, and go limp when they're done.

Every corner of the fair whirls with light and jumps with sound.

From a distance, it is a small town of tents

and pumpkins and tractors and carousels and cows.

The smell of fried dough fills the evening.

Late that night, a farmer picks up trash.

Tents come down slowly around her,

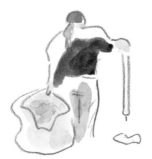

sighing as air whooshes out of them.

Animals look at her sideways as they parade  onto trucks.

One calf ignores her and rolls in dirt.

The next morning, the field is empty again. The last food has been eaten, the last ride taken,

the last pie judged. Ribbons have been awarded, and the final pig has been loaded away.

The fair is over.

blue hills

For all my goats

Watercolors and pencil were used for the full-color art.
The text was hand lettered by the artist.

Printed in Singapore by Tien Wah Press
First Edition 10 9 8 7 6 5 4 3 2 1

Library of Congress Cataloging-in-Publication Data
Cooper, Elisha.
Country fair / by Elisha Cooper.
p. cm.
Summary: Describes the activities that go on at
a country fair, from the animal exhibits, food tasting,
and ox pulls to a wood chopping exhibition.
ISBN 0-688-15531-6
[1. Fairs.] I. Title.
PZ7.C784737Co 1997 [E]—dc21
96-52583 CIP AC